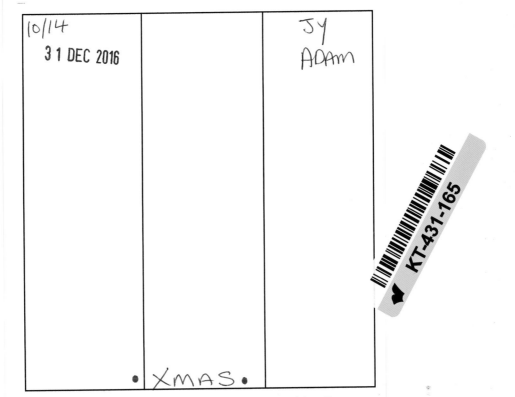

10/14 3 1 DEC 2016		JY ADAM
	• XMAS •	

First published in Great Britain in 1996
by Orion Children's Books
First published in paperback in 1997
Reissued 2014 by Orion Children's Books
a division of the Orion Publishing Group Ltd
Orion House
5 Upper Saint Martin's Lane
London WC2H 9EA

A Hachette UK Company

1 3 5 7 9 10 8 6 4 2

Text © Georgie Adams 1996
Illustrations © Selina Young 1996

The moral right of Georgie Adams and Selina Young
to be identified as author and illustrator
of this work has been asserted.

The Orion Publishing Group's policy is to use papers that are natural,
renewable and recyclable products and made from wood grown in
sustainable forests. The logging and manufacturing processes are expected to
conform to the environmental regulations of the country of origin.
A catalogue record for this book is available from the British Library.

Printed in China

Hardback ISBN 978 1 4440 1211 8
Paperback ISBN 978 1 4440 1212 5

www.orionbook.co.uk

*For my brood –
Abigail and Imogen –
with love G.A.*

Nanny Fox and the THREE LITTLE PIGS

Georgie Adams + Selina Young

Orion
Children's Books

It was Christmas Eve and Arnold Fox was helping the chicks
wrap presents.

Mrs Buff Orpington was keeping a beady eye out for foxes.
It was about this time last year that the next-door hens
had gone missing.

With Arnold, of course, it was different. She had taken a risk
letting him look after her chicks, but he was the perfect nanny.
Arnold was the only fox she could trust.

When all the gifts were wrapped, Arnold and the chicks set
off round the farmyard.

They visited the goats, the geese and the cows.
There was a parcel for each of them.

"Just three presents left," said Arnold.

"Who could they be for?"

"The three little pigs!" cheeped the chicks.

The piglets opened their parcels with squeals of delight.

But when Arnold said goodbye, the little pigs looked sad.

"Please stay," said one.

"We could play Three Little Pigs," said another.

"You could be the Big Bad Wolf!" said the third.

The chicks couldn't imagine Nanny Fox as a wicked wolf.

He was much too kind and gentle.

"I could wear a mask," said Arnold.

"We'll help you make one!" said the chicks.

So Arnold and the chicks played all afternoon.
They made a fierce-looking mask with sharp teeth
and a long, pink tongue.

The piglets made pretend houses of straw, sticks and bricks.
Every time Arnold said,

"Little pig, little pig, let me come in,"

the little pigs sang,

"No, not by the hair on my chinny chin chin!"
"Then," said Arnold in his Big Bad Wolf voice,

"I'll huff and I'll puff, and I'll
blow your house in!"

Arnold looked very frightening. But the little pigs knew it was
Nanny Fox, so they laughed.

At bedtime in the henhouse, Arnold read the chicks
the story of *The Three Little Pigs*. He pretended to be the Big
Bad Wolf over and over again.

Arnold's family, who lived in the woods, had been thinking
about Arnold and the chicks.

"If we want chicken for dinner," said Ma Fox,
"we'll have to go up to the farm."
"Arnold's there now," said Pa Fox. "It won't be easy."

"We could disguise ourselves," said Lucy.

"What as?" said Dennis. "Worms?"

"No silly!" snapped Lucy.

"Pa could dress up as Father Christmas and we could be reindeer!"

"I'll take a big sack for the hens," chuckled Pa.

"I'll wait here with a cooking pot!" said Ma.

"When?" said Dennis.

"Tonight," said Lucy. "It's Christmas Eve!"

Arnold's family got busy. Ma Fox helped Lucy and Dennis
with their reindeer costumes.

Back at the farm all seemed safe and quiet,
until Mrs Buff Orpington heard footsteps crunching through
the snow and saw three shadowy shapes.

"Who's there?" she said.

"Father Christmas," said a voice. It was Pa Fox.

"Well, where are your reindeer?" said Mrs Buff Orpington.

"Here!" said Dennis and Lucy.

"Only two?" said Mrs Buff Orpington.

"The others couldn't come," said Lucy, trying not to giggle.

Mrs Buff Orpington took a closer look at Father Christmas.

"What have you got in your sack?"

"Nothing yet," said Pa Fox, flinging back his hood.

"But YOU can go in first!"

Mrs Buff Orpington screeched and squawked as the two reindeer bundled her into the sack.

"Stop flapping!" said Lucy.

"And pecking!" said Dennis, rubbing his nose.

Mrs Buff Orpington's squawks could be heard all over the farmyard. The goats, the geese, the cows and the three little pigs hurried to see what was the matter.

In the henhouse the chicks jumped from their beds
and hid behind the door.

Then Arnold, who was still wearing his wolf mask,
sprang to the rescue.

Well! The sight of those sharp teeth and long, pink tongue
gave Pa Fox the fright of his life.

"I'm going to GOBBLE YOU UP!"

growled Arnold in his Big Bad Wolf voice.

Dennis and Lucy took one look,
dropped the sack and ran!
Pa Fox tripped over his beard
and rolled all the way
back to the woods.

Everyone cheered. And Arnold took a bow.

Just then Mrs Buff Orpington poked her head out of the sack.

"When you've all finished," she squawked, "I should like some help! Huh! Father Christmas and two reindeer. They didn't trick me for a minute!"

Arnold tried not to smile.

"Of course not," he said.

"Now let's all go to bed, then the real
Father Christmas will come!"